all-time great classics

The Lord of The Flies

(A masterpiece of William Golding)

MANOJ PUBLICATIONS

Publishers :

MANOJ PUBLICATIONS

761, Main Road, Burari, Delhi-110084 (INDIA)

Mobile : 09999476076, 09868112194
08178823569, 08178854810

E-mail : info@manojpublications.com

For online shopping visit our website :
www.sawanonlinebookstore.com

From the Publisher's Desk

In this age of competition, none has the time to go through long novels which seem to have no endings. Maybe these kinds of novels were written during the time when people led leisurely life. They had plenty of time at their disposal. Reading good literary work on weekend was the main source of entertainment. Now the time has entirely changed. Readers search for short, excellent literary works which are comprised of well-designed illustrations. These illustrations clear their themes at very first glance. As a reader flips through the pages of an illustrated novel, each chapter unfolds in a very easy and interesting style.

Keeping this modern approach in mind, we have brought out this novel in a very novel way. Easy-to-understand language accompanied by life-like illustrations has added four-fold beauty to the novel. At the end of the novel, questions based on each and every chapter have been given to test the mental faculty of the reader.

All these outstanding features incorporated in this novel have made it suitable for young and old alike. Undoubtedly, it is ideal for classrooms, library and personal collection too.

About the Author

Sir William Gerald Golding was born on 19th Sep 1911, Newquay, Cornwall, England, U.K. His father was a science master at Marlborough Grammar School. The young Golding and his elder brother Joseph attended the school where their father taught. Their mother Mildred kept house. Golding took his B.A. (Hons) Second Class in the summer of 1934.

His first book 'Poems' was published in London. He married Ann Brookfield, an analytic chemist, on 30th Sep 1939. He even offered his services during the Second World War. In 1985, he and his wife moved to Tullimear House at Perranarworthal near Truro, Cornwall, where he died of heart failure.

He was an English novelist, poet, playwright. He won Nobel Prize for literature. He is best known for his novel 'The Lord of the Flies'. He was also awarded the Booker Prize for literature in 1980 for his novel Rites Of Passage, the first book of the trilogy To The Ends Of The Earth. Having been appointed a CBE in 1966, Golding was knighted by Queen Elizabeth II at Buckingham Palace in 1988.

In 2008, The Times ranked Golding third on their list of the 50 greatest British writers since 1945.

Contents

Ralph (a boy of thirteen) ***Piggy (the fat boy)***

Sam (a boy of ten) ***Eric (a boy of twelve)***

Ralph on an Uninhabited Island

Ralph was a British boy. One day, he along with his family was sailing. A violent storm took place and their ship was blown off ashore. When Ralph opened his eyes, he found himself on an island. The island was uninhabited. His family was nowhere to be seen. Now Ralph had no alternative but to delve deep into the island and enjoy its scenic beauty. So, he garnered some courage and proceeded towards the interior of the island. All of a sudden, a voice came from behind him. He was somewhat scared.

He shook his head and increased his speed. Then he tripped over a branch and came down with a crash.

A fat boy stood by him, breathing hard.

"My auntie told me not to run," he explained, "on account of my asthma."

"That's right. Can't catch my breath. I was the only boy in our school what had asthma," said the fat boy with a touch of pride, "And I've been wearing specs since I was three."

He took off his glasses and held them out to Ralph, blinking and smiling, and then started to wipe them against his grubby wind-breaker.

He put on his glasses, waded away from Ralph, and crouched down among the tangled foliage.

"I'll be out again in just a minute."

He wiped his glasses and adjusted them on his button nose.

Ralph disentangled himself cautiously and stole away through the branches. In a few seconds the fat boy's grunts were behind him and he was hurrying towards the screen that still lay between him and the lagoon. He climbed over a broken trunk and was out of the jungle.

Ralph was old enough, twelve years and a few months, to have lost the prominent tummy of childhood and not yet old enough for adolescence to have made him awkward.

"Ralph–"

The fat boy lowered himself over the terrace and sat down carefully, using the edge as a seat.

He wiped his glasses and adjusted them on his button nose. The frame had made a deep, pink "V" on the bridge. He looked critically at Ralph's golden body and then down at his own clothes. He laid a hand on the end of a zipper that extended down his chest.

"My auntie–"

Then he opened the zipper with decision and pulled the whole wind-breaker over his head.

Ralph looked at him sidelong and said nothing.

As the hours passed by, they because good friends. They played on the island and enjoyed themselves all the scenic beauty of the island. Soon they were joined by some other boys of their ages. They were all grown-ups. The fat boy and Ralph who sometimes called the fat boy 'Piggy', welcomed the boys with open arms. First of all, Ralph introduced himself and the fat boy to the boys who felt very elated at finding new friends in that uninhabited island.

Their names were Sam, Eric, Henry and Jack Merridew, to name a few. All the friends were happy and had fun and frolic. A storm of laughter arose and even the tiniest child joined in. For the moment the boys were a closed circuit of sympathy with Piggy outside: he went very pink, bowed his head and cleaned his glasses again.

Finally the laughter died away and the naming continued. There was Maurice, next in size among the choir boys to Jack, but broad and grinning all the time. There was a slight, furtive boy whom no one knew, who kept to himself with an inner intensity of avoidance and secrecy. He muttered that his name was Roger and was silent again. Bill, Robert, Harold, Henry; the choir boy who had fainted sat up against a palm trunk, smiled pallidly at Ralph and said that his name was Simon.

Jack spoke.

"We've got to decide about being rescued."

There was a buzz. One of the small boys, Henry, said that he wanted to go home.

"Shut up," said Ralph absently. He lifted the conch. "Seems to me we ought to have a chief to decide things."

"A chief! A chief!"

"I ought to be chief," said Jack with simple arrogance, "because I'm chapter chorister and head boy. I can sing C sharp."

"Well then," said Jack, "I–"

He hesitated. The dark boy, Roger, stirred at last and spoke up.

"Let's have a vote."

"Yes!"

"Vote for chief!"

"Let's vote–"

Ralph raised a hand for silence.

"All right. Who wants Jack for chief?"

With dreary obedience the choir raised their hands.

"Who wants me?"

Every hand outside the choir except Piggy's was raised immediately. Then Piggy, too, raised his hand grudgingly into the air.

Ralph counted.

"I'm chief then."

The circle of boys broke into applause. Even the choir applauded; and the freckles on Jack's face disappeared under a blush of mortification. He started up, then changed his mind and sat down again while the air rang. Ralph looked at him, eager to offer something.

❐

A Blazing Fire

All the boys had appointed Ralph their chief. All were happy with Ralph as their chief. Ralph had to decide the future course of action.

He said "We're on an island. We've been on the mountain top and seen water all round. We saw no houses, no smoke, no footprints, no boats, no people. We're on an uninhabited island with no other people on it."

Jack broke in.

"All the same you need an army–for hunting. Hunting pigs–"

"Yes. There are pigs on the island."

He lifted the shell on his knees and looked round the sun-slashed faces.

"There aren't any grown-ups. We shall have to look after ourselves."

Below the other side of the mountain top was a platform of forest.

"Down there we could get as much wood as we want."

Jack nodded and pulled at his underlip. Starting perhaps a hundred feet below them on the steeper side of the mountain, the patch might have been designed expressly for fuel.

Trees, forced by the damp heat, found too little soil for full growth, fell early and decayed: creepers cradled

All were happy with Ralph as their chief.

them, and new saplings searched a way up. Jack turned to the choir, who stood ready. Their black caps of maintenance were slid over one ear like berets.

"We'll build a pile. Come on."

They found the likeliest path down and began tugging at the dead wood. And the small boys who had reached the top came sliding too till everyone but Piggy was busy. Most of the wood was so rotten that when they pulled, it broke up into a shower of fragments and woodlice and decay; but some trunks came out in one piece.

The twins, Sam and Eric, were the first to get a likely log but they could do nothing till Ralph, Jack, Simon, Roger and Maurice found room for a hand-hold. Then they inched the grotesque dead thing up the rock and toppled it over on top. Each party of boys added a quota, less or more, and the pile grew. At the return Ralph found himself alone on a limb with Jack and they grinned at each other, sharing this burden.

Once more, amid the breeze, the shouting, the slanting sunlight on the high mountain, was shed that glamour, that strange invisible light of friendship, adventure, and content.

All the friends collected a huge heap of dead wood and gave it fire. Lo and behold! In a few minutes' time the dead wood being completely dry began to turn into a blaze. The boys felt very elated. They started dancing around the blazing fire.

The trees were so rootles and now so tinger dry that whole limbs yielded passionately to the yellow flames that powered upwards and shook a great beard of flame twenty feet in the air. For yards round the fire the heat was like a blow and the breeze was a river of sparks.

Trunks crumbled to white dust. All the boys got scared and worried.

A tree exploded in the fire like a bomb. Tall swathes of creepers rose for a moment into view, agonized, and went down again. The little boys screamed at them.

"Snakes! Snakes! Look at the snakes!"

In the west, and unheeded, the sun lay only an inch or two above the sea. Their faces were lit redly from beneath. Piggy fell against a rock and clutched it with both hands.

❐

Chapter 3

Beasts from Water and Air

As a result of huge and explosive fire the grass was worn away in front of each trunk but grew tall and untrodden in the centre of the triangle. Then, at the apex, the grass was thick again because no one sat there. All round the place of assembly the grey trunks rose, straight or leaning, and supported the low roof of leaves. On two sides was the beach; behind, the lagoon; in front, the darkness of the island.

Ralph turned to the chief's seat. They had never had an assembly as late before. That was why the place looked so different. Normally the underside of the green roof was lit by a tangle of golden reflections, and their faces were lit upside down–like, thought Ralph, when you hold an electric torch in your hands. But now the sun was slanting in at one side, so that the shadows were where they ought to be.

Again, he fell into that strange mood of speculation that was so foreign to him.

Ralph moved impatiently. The trouble was, if you were a chief you had to think, you had to be wise. And then the occasion slipped by so that you had to grab at a decision.

Ralph went on.

"We have lots of assemblies. Everybody enjoys speaking and being together. We decide things. But they don't get done. We were going to have water brought from the stream and left in those coconut shells under fresh leaves. So it was, for a few days. Now there's no water. The shells are dry. People drink from the river."

Piggy took the conch out of his hands. His voice was indignant.

"I don't believe in any ghosts–ever!"

Jack was up too, unaccountably angry.

"Who cares what you believe–Fatty!"

"I got the conch!"

There was the sound of a brief tussle and the conch moved to and fro.

Ralph pushed between them and got a thump on the chest. He wrestled the conch from someone and sat down breathlessly.

"There's too much talk about ghosts. We ought to have left all this for daylight."

A hushed and anonymous voice broke in.

"Perhaps that's what the beast is–a ghost."

The assembly was shaken as by a wind.

He gave a wild whoop and leapt down to the pale sand. At once the platform was full of noise and excitement, scramblings, screams and laughter. The assembly shredded away and became a discursive and random scatter from the palms to the water and away along the beach, beyond night-sight. Ralph found his cheek touching the conch and took it from Piggy.

The dispersed figures had come together on the sand and were a dense black mass that revolved. They were chanting something and littluns that had had enough were staggering away, howling. Ralph raised the conch to his lips and then lowered it.

"The trouble is: Are there ghosts, Piggy? Or beasts?"

The dancing, chanting boys had worked themselves away till their sound was nothing but a wordless rhythm.

Ralph shuddered violently and moved closer to Piggy, so that they bumped frighteningly.

A thin wail out of the darkness chilled them and set them grabbing for each other. Then the wail rose, remote and unearthly, and turned to an inarticulate gibbering.

There was no light left save that of the stars. When they had understood what made this ghostly noise and Percival was quiet again, Ralph and Simon picked him up unhandily and carried him to a shelter. Piggy hung about near for all his brave words, and the three bigger boys went together to the next shelter. They lay restlessly and noisily among the dry leaves, watching the patch of stars that was the opening towards the lagoon.

A sliver of moon rose over the horizon, hardly large enough to make a path of light even when it sat right down on the water; but there were other lights in the sky, that moved fast, winked, or went out, though not even a faint popping came down from the battle fought at ten miles' height.

In the darkness of early morning there were noises by a rock a little way down the side of the mountain. Two boys rolled out a pile of brushwood and dead leaves, two dim shadows talking sleepily to each other. They were the twins, on duty at the fire. In theory one should have been asleep and one on watch. But they could never manage to do things sensibly if that meant acting independently, and since staying awake all night was impossible, they had both gone to sleep. Now they approached the darker smudge that had been the signal fire, yawning, rubbing their eyes, treading with practised feet. When they reached it they stopped yawning, and one ran quickly back for brushwood and leaves.

Ralph was dreaming. He had fallen asleep after what seemed hours of tossing and turning noisily among the dry leaves. Even the sounds of nightmare from the other shelters no longer reached him, for he was back to where he came from, feeding the ponies with sugar over the garden wall. Then someone was shaking his arm, telling him that it was time for tea.

They lay there listening, at first with doubt but then with terror to the description the twins breathed at them between bouts of extreme silence. Soon the darkness was full of claws, full of the awful unknown and menace. An interminable dawn faded the stars out, and at last light, sad and grey, filtered into the shelter. They began to stir though still the world outside the shelter was impossibly dangerous. The maze of the darkness sorted into near and far, and at the high point of the sky the cloudlets were warmed with color. A single sea bird flapped upwards with a hoarse cry that was echoed presently, and something squawked in the forest. Now streaks of cloud near the horizon began to glow rosily, and the feathery tops of the palms were green.

Ralph knelt in the entrance to the shelter and peered cautiously round him.

Ralph took the conch from where it lay on the polished seat and held it to his lips; but then he hesitated and did not blow. He held the shell up instead and showed it to them and they understood.

The rays of the sun that were fanning upwards from below the horizon swung downwards to eye-level. Ralph looked for a moment at the growing slice of gold that lit them from the right hand and seemed to make

The circle of boys shrank away in horror.

speech possible. The circle of boys before him bristled with hunting spears.

He handed the conch to Eric, the nearest of the twins.

The circle of boys shrank away in horror. Johnny, yawning still, burst into noisy tears and was slapped by Bill till he choked on them. The bright morning was full of threats and the circle began to change. It faced out, rather than in, and the spears of sharpened wood were like a fence. Jack called them back to the centre.

The rest of the boys watched intently. Piggy, finding himself uncomfortably embroiled, slid the conch to Ralph's knees and sat down. The silence grew oppressive and Piggy held his breath.

"This is more than a hunter's job," said Ralph at last, "because you can't track the beast. And don't you want to be rescued?"

Ralph parted the screen of grass and looked out. There were only a few more yards of stony ground and then the two sides of the island came almost together so that one expected a peak of headland. But instead of this a narrow ledge of rock, a few yards wide and perhaps fifteen long, continued the island out into the sea. There lay another of those pieces of pink squareness that underlay the structure of the island. This side of the castle, perhaps a hundred feet high, was the pink bastion they had seen from the mountain-top. The rock of the cliff was split and the top littered with great lumps that seemed to totter.

Behind Ralph the tall grass had filled with silent hunters. Ralph looked at Jack.

"You're a hunter."

Jack went red.

"I know. All right."

Something deep in Ralph spoke for him.

"I'm chief. I'll go. Don't argue."

He turned to the others.

He was surrounded on all sides by chasms of empty air. There was nowhere to hide, even if one did not have to go on. He paused on the narrow neck and looked down. Soon, in a matter of centuries, the sea would make an island of the castle. On the right hand was the lagoon, troubled by the open sea; and on the left–Ralph shuddered. The lagoon had protected them from the Pacific: and for some reason only Jack had gone right down to the water on the other side. Now he saw the landsman's view of the swell and it seemed like the breathing of some stupendous creature.

Slowly the waters sank among the rocks, revealing pink tables of granite, strange growths of coral, polyp, and weed. Down, down, the waters went, whispering like the wind among the heads of the forest. There was one flat rock there, spread like a table, and the waters sucking down on the four weedy sides made them seem like cliffs. Then the sleeping leviathan breathed out, the waters rose, the weed streamed, and the water boiled over the table rock with a roar. There was no sense of the passage of waves; only this minute-long fall and rise and fall.

Ralph turned away to the red cliff. They were waiting behind him in the long grass, waiting to see what he would do. He noticed that the sweat in his palm was cool now; realized with surprise that he did not really expect to meet any beast and didn't know what he would do about it if he did.

The clamour broke out. Some of the boys wanted to go back to the beach. Some wanted to roll more rocks.

The sun was bright and danger had faded with the darkness.

"Jack. The beast might be on the other side. You can lead again. You've been."

"We could go by the shore. There's fruit."

Bill came up to Ralph.

"Why can't we stay here for a bit?"

"That's right."

"Let's have a fort."

"There's no food here," said Ralph, "and no shelter. Not much fresh water."

"This would make a wizard fort."

"We can roll rocks."

"Right onto the bridge."

"I say we'll go on!" shouted Ralph furiously. "We've got to make certain. We'll go now."

"Let's stay here."

"Back to the shelter."

"I'm tired."

"No!"

Ralph struck the skin off his knuckles. They did not seem to hurt.

❒

Coming across Strange Creatures

Here, on the other side of the island, the view was utterly different. The filmy enchantments of mirage could not endure the cold ocean water and the horizon was hard, clipped blue. Ralph wandered down to the rocks.

Wave after wave, Ralph followed the rise and fall until something of the remoteness of the sea numbed his brain. Then gradually the almost infinite size of this water forced itself on his attention. This was the divider, the barrier. On the other side of the island, swathed at midday with mirage, defended by the shield of the quiet lagoon, one might dream of rescue; but here, faced by the brute obtuseness of the ocean, the miles of division, one was clamped down, one was helpless and one was condemned.

Simon was speaking almost in his ear. Ralph found that he had rock painfully gripped in both hands, found his body arched, the muscles of his neck stiff, his mouth strained open.

The bushes crashed ahead of them. Boys flung themselves wildly from the pig track and scrabbled in the creepers, screaming. Ralph saw Jack nudged aside and fall. Then there was a creature bounding along the pig track toward him, with tusks gleaming and an intimidating grunt. Ralph found he was able to measure the distance coldly and take aim. With the boar only five yards away, he flung the foolish wooden stick that he carried, saw it hit the great snout and hang there for a moment. The boar's note changed to a squeal and it swerved aside into the covert. The pig-run filled with shouting boys again, Jack came running back, and poked about in the undergrowth.

Once more Ralph dreamed, letting his skilful feet deal with the difficulties of the path. Yet here his feet seemed less skillful than before. For most of the way they were forced right down to the bare rock by the water and had to edge along between that and the dark luxuriance of the forest. There were little cliffs to be scaled, some to be used as paths, lengthy traverses where one used hands as well as feet. Here and there they could clamber over wave-wet rock, leaping across clear pools that the tide had left. They came to a gully that split the narrow foreshore like a defense. This seemed to have no bottom and they peered awe-stricken into the gloomy crack where water gurgled. Then the wave came back, the gully boiled before them and spray dashed up to the very creeper so that the boys were wet and shrieking. They tried the forest but it was thick and woven like a bird's nest. In the end they had to jump one by one, waiting till the water sank; and even so, some of them got a second drenching. After that the rocks seemed to be growing impassable so they sat for a time, letting their rags dry and watching the clipped outlines of the rollers that moved so slowly past the island. They found fruit in a haunt of bright little birds that hovered like insects. Then Ralph said they were

He himself climbed a tree.

going too slowly. He himself climbed a tree and parted the canopy, and saw the square head of the mountain seeming still a great way off. Then they tried to hurry along the rocks and Robert cut his knee quite badly and they had to recognize that this path must be taken slowly if they were to be safe. So they proceeded after that as if they were climbing a dangerous mountain, until the rocks became an uncompromising cliff, overhung with impossible jungle and falling sheer into the sea.

Ralph looked at the sun critically.

The pig-track was a dark tunnel, for the sun was sliding quickly toward the edge of the world and in the forest shadows were never far to seek. The track was broad and beaten and they ran along at a swift trot. Then the roof of leaves broke up and they halted, breathing quickly, looking at the few stars that pricked round the head of the mountain.

Their footsteps and the occasional breeze were stirring up small devils of dust. Now that they stopped again, Ralph had time while he coughed to remember how silly they were. If there was no beast–and almost certainly there was no beast–in that case, well and good; but if there was something waiting on top of the mountain– what was the use of three of them, handicapped by the darkness and carrying only sticks?

Ralph felt his knee against something hard and rocked a charred trunk that was edgy to the touch. He felt the sharp cinders that had been bark push against the back of his knee and knew that Roger had sat down. He felt with his hands and lowered himself beside Roger, while the trunk rocked among invisible ashes. Roger, uncommunicative by nature, said nothing. He offered no opinion on the beast nor told Ralph why he had chosen to come on this mad expedition. He simply sat and rocked the trunk gently. Ralph noticed a rapid and infuriating tapping noise and realized that Roger was banging his silly wooden stick against something.

So they sat, the rocking, tapping, impervious Roger and Ralph, fuming; round them the close sky was loaded with stars, save where the mountain punched up a hole of blackness.

There was a slithering noise high above them, the sound of someone taking giant and dangerous strides on rock or ash. Then Jack found them, and was shivering and croaking in a voice they could just recognize as his.

"I saw a thing on top."

They heard him blunder against the trunk which rocked violently. He lay silent for a moment, then muttered.

"Keep a good lookout. It may be following."

A shower of ash pattered round them. Jack sat up.

"I saw a thing bulge on the mountain."

"You only imagined it," said Ralph shakily, "because nothing would bulge. Not any sort of creature."

Roger spoke; they jumped, for they had forgotten him.

"A frog."

Jack giggled and shuddered.

"Some frog. There was a noise too. A kind of 'plop' noise. Then the thing bulged."

Ralph surprised himself, not so much by the quality of his voice, which was even, but by the bravado of its intention.

"We'll go and look."

They crept forward, Roger lagging a little. Jack and Ralph turned the shoulder of the mountain together. The glittering lengths of the lagoon lay below them and beyond that a long white smudge that was the reef. Roger joined them.

Jack whispered.

"Let's creep forward on hands and knees. Maybe it's asleep."

Roger and Ralph moved on, this time leaving Jack in the rear, for all his brave words. They came to the flat top where the rock was hard to hands and knees.

A creature that bulged.

Ralph put his hand in the cold, soft ashes of the fire and smothered a cry. His hand and shoulder were twitching from the unlooked-for contact. Green lights of nausea appeared for a moment and ate into the darkness. Roger lay behind him and Jack's mouth was at his ear.

Ashes blew into Ralph's face from the dead fire. He could not see the gap or anything else, because the green lights were opening again and growing, and the top of the mountain was sliding sideways.

Once more, from a distance, he heard Jack's whisper.

"Scared?"

Not scared so much as paralyzed; hung up there immovable on the top of a diminishing, moving mountain. Jack slid away from him, Roger bumped, fumbled with a hiss of breath, and passed onwards. He heard them whispering.

"Can you see anything?"

In front of them, only three or four yards away, was a rock-like hump where no rock should be. Ralph could hear a tiny chattering noise coming from somewhere—perhaps from his own mouth. He bound himself together with his will, fused his fear and loathing into a hatred, and stood up. He took two leaden steps forward.

Behind them the silver of moon had drawn clear of the horizon. Before them, something like a great ape was sitting asleep with its head between its knees. Then the wind roared in the forest, there was confusion in the darkness and the creature lifted its head, holding toward them the ruin of a face.

Ralph found himself taking giant strides among the ashes, heard other creatures crying out and leaping and dared the impossible on the dark slope; presently the mountain was deserted, save for the three abandoned sticks and the thing that bowed.

❒

Chapter 5

Darkness All Around

Piggy looked up miserably from the dawn-pale beach to the dark mountain.

"Are you sure? Really sure, I mean?"

I told you a dozen times now," said Ralph, "We saw it."

"Did you think we're safe down here?"

"How the hell should I know?"

Ralph jerked away from him and walked a few paces along the beach. Jack was kneeling and drawing a circular pattern in the sand with his forefinger. Piggy's voice came to them, hushed.

"Are you sure? Really?"

"Go up and see," said Jack contemptuously, "and good riddance."

"No fear."

"The beast had teeth," said Ralph, "and big black eyes."

He shuddered violently. Piggy took off his one round of glass and polished the surface.

"What we going to do?" Ralph turned toward the platform. The conch glimmered among the trees, a white blob against the place where the sun would rise. He pushed back his mop.

"I don't know."

He remembered the panic flight down the

mountainside. "I don't think we'd ever fight a thing that size, honestly, you know. We'd talk but we wouldn't fight a tiger. We'd hide. Even Jack would hide."

Jack still looked at the sand.

"What about my hunters?"

Simon came stealing out of the shadows by the shelters. Ralph ignored Jack's question. He pointed to the touch of yellow above the sea.

"As long as there's light we're brave enough. But then? And now that thing squats by the fire as though it didn't want us to be rescued."

He was twisting his hands now, unconsciously. His voice rose.

"So we can't have a signal fire. We're beaten."

A point of gold appeared above the sea and at once all the sky lightened.

"What about my hunters?"

"Boys armed with sticks."

Jack got to his feet. His face was red as he marched away. Piggy put on his one glass and looked at Ralph.

"Now you done it. You been rude about his hunters."

"Oh shut up!"

The sound of the inexpertly blown conch interrupted them. As though he were serenading the rising sun, Jack went on blowing till the shelters were astir and the hunters crept to the platform and the littluns whimpered as now they so frequently did. Ralph rose obediently, and Piggy, and they went to the platform.

"Talk," said Ralph bitterly, "talk, talk, talk."

He took the conch from Jack.

"This meeting–"

Jack interrupted him.

"I called it."

"If you hadn't called it I should have. You just blew the conch."

"Well, isn't that calling it?"

"Oh, take it! Go on–talk!"

Ralph thrust the conch into Jack's arms and sat down on the trunk.

"I've called an assembly," said Jack, "because of a lot of things. First, you know now, we've seen the beast. We crawled up. We were only a few feet away. The beast sat up and looked at us. I don't know what it does. We don't even know what it is."

"The beast comes out of the sea."

"Out of the dark–"

"Trees–"

"Quiet!" shouted Jack. "You, listen. The beast is sitting up there, whatever it is."

"Perhaps it's waiting."

"Hunting–"

"Yes, hunting."

"Hunting," said Jack. He remembered his age-old tremors in the forest. "Yes. The beast is a hunter. Only–shut up! The next thing is that we couldn't kill it. And the next is that Ralph said my hunters are no good."

"I never said that!"

"I've got the conch. Ralph thinks you're cowards, running away from the boar and the beast. And that's not all."

There was a kind of sigh on the platform as if everyone knew what was coming. Jack's voice went up, tremulous yet determined, pushing against the uncooperative silence.

"He's like Piggy. He says things like Piggy. He isn't a proper chief."

The two boys glared at each other through screens of hair.

Jack clutched the conch to him.

"He's a coward himself."

For a moment he paused and then went on.

"On top, when Roger and me went on–he stayed back."

"I went too!"

"After."

The two boys glared at each other through screens of hair.

"I went on too," said Ralph, "then I ran away. So did you."

"Call me a coward then."

Jack turned to the hunters.

"He's not a hunter. He'd never have got us meat. He isn't a prefect and we don't know anything about him. He just gives orders and expects people to obey for nothing. All this talk–"

"All this talk!" shouted Ralph. "Talk, talk! Who wanted it? Who called the meeting?"

Jack turned, red in the face, his chin sunk back. He glowered up under his eyebrows.

"All right then," he said in tones of deep meaning, and menace, "all right."

He held the conch against his chest with one hand and stabbed the air with his index finger.

"Who thinks Ralph oughtn't to be chief?"

He looked expectantly at the boys ranged round, who had frozen. Under the palms there was deadly silence.

"Hands up," said Jack strongly, "whoever wants Ralph not to be chief?"

The silence continued, breathless and heavy and full of shame. Slowly the red drained from Jack's cheeks, then came back with a painful rush. He licked his lips and turned his head at an angle, so that his gaze avoided the embarrassment of linking with another's eye.

"How many think–"

His voice tailed off. The hands that held the conch shook. He cleared his throat, and spoke loudly.

"All right then."

He laid the conch with great care in the grass at his feet. The humiliating tears were running from the corner of each eye.

"I'm not going to play any longer. Not with you."

Most of the boys were looking down now, at the grass or their feet. Jack cleared his throat again.

"I'm not going to be a part of Ralph's lot."

He looked along the right-hand logs, numbering the hunters that had been a choir.

"I'm going off by myself. He can catch his own pigs. Anyone who wants to hunt when I do can come too."

He blundered out of the triangle towards the drop to the white sand.

"Jack!"

Jack turned and looked back at Ralph. For a moment he paused and then cried out, high-pitched, enraged.

"No!"

He leapt down from the platform and ran along the beach, paying no heed to the steady fall of his tears; and until he dived into the forest Ralph watched him.

Piggy was indignant.

"I been talking, Ralph, and you just stood there like."

Softly, looking at Piggy and not seeing him, Ralph spoke to himself.

"He'll come back. When the sun goes down he'll come." He looked at the conch in Piggy's hand.

"What?"

"Well there!"

Piggy gave up the attempt to rebuke Ralph. He polished his glass again and went back to his subject.

"We can do without Jack Merridew. There's others besides him on this island. But now we really got a beast, though I can't hardly believe it, we'll need to stay close to the platform; there'll be less need of him and his hunting. So now we can really decide on what's what."

"There's no help, Piggy. Nothing to be done."

For a while they sat in depressed silence. Then Simon stood up and took the conch from Piggy, who was so astonished that he remained on his feet. Ralph looked up at Simon.

"Simon? What is it this time?"

A half-sound of jeering ran round the circle and Simon shrank from it.

"I thought there might be something to do. Something we-"

Again the pressure of the assembly took his voice away. He sought for help and sympathy and chose Piggy. He turned half toward him, clutching the conch to his brown chest.

"I think we ought to climb the mountain."

The circle shivered with dread. Simon broke off and turned to Piggy who was looking at him with an expression of derisive incomprehension.

"What's the good of climbing up to this here beast when Ralph and the other two couldn't do nothing?"

Simon whispered his answer.

"What else is there to do?"

His speech made, he allowed Piggy to lift the conch

out of his hands. Then he retired and sat as far away from the others as possible.

Piggy was speaking now with more assurance and with what, if the circumstances had not been so serious, the others would have recognized as pleasure.

"I said we could all do without a certain person. Now I say we got to decide on what can be done. And I think I could tell you what Ralph's going to say next. The most important thing on the island is the smoke and you can't have no smoke without a fire."

Ralph made a restless movement.

"No go, Piggy. We've got no fire. That thing sits up there–we'll have to stay here."

Piggy lifted the conch as though to add power to his next words.

"We got no fire on the mountain. But what's wrong with a fire down here? A fire could be built on them rocks. On the sand, even. We'd make smoke just the same."

"That's right!"

"Smoke!"

"By the bathing pool!"

The boys began to babble. Only Piggy could have the intellectual daring to suggest moving the fire from the mountain.

"So we'll have the fire down here," said Ralph. He looked about him. "We can build it just here between the bathing pool and the platform. Of course–"

He broke off, frowning, thinking the thing out, unconsciously tugging at the stub of a nail with his teeth.

"Of course the smoke won't show so much, not be seen so far away. But we needn't go near, near the–"

The others nodded in perfect comprehension. There would be no need to go near.

"We'll build the fire now."

The greatest ideas are the simplest. Now there was something to be done they worked with passion. Piggy was so full of delight and expanding liberty in Jack's departure, so full of pride in his contribution to the good of society, that he helped to fetch wood. The wood he fetched was close at hand, a fallen tree on the platform that they did not need for the assembly, yet to the others the sanctity of the platform had protected even what was useless there. Then the twins realized they would have a fire near them as a comfort in the night and this set a few littluns dancing and clapping hands.

The wood was not so dry as the fuel they had used on the mountain. Much of it was damply rotten and full of insects that scurried; logs had to be lifted from the soil with care or they crumbled into sodden powder. More than this, in order to avoid going deep into the forest the boys worked near at hand on any fallen wood no matter how tangled with new growth. The skirts of the forest and the scar were familiar, near the conch and the shelters and sufficiently friendly in daylight. What they might become in darkness nobody cared to think.

They worked therefore with great energy and cheerfulness, though as time crept by there was a suggestion of panic in the energy and hysteria in the cheerfulness. They built a pyramid of leaves and twigs, branches and logs, on the bare sand by the platform. For the first time on the island, Piggy himself removed his one glass, knelt down and focused the sun on tinder. Soon there was a ceiling of smoke and a bush of yellow flame.

The littluns who had seen few fires since the first catastrophe became wildly excited. They danced and sang and there was a partyish air about the gathering.

At last Ralph stopped work and stood up, smudging the sweat from his face with a dirty forearm.

"We'll have to have a small fire. This one's too big to keep up."

Piggy sat down carefully on the sand and began to polish his glass.

"We could experiment. We could find out how to make a small hot fire and then put green branches on to make smoke. Some of them leaves must be better for that than the others."

As the fire died down so did the excitement. The littluns stopped singing and dancing and drifted away toward the sea or the fruit trees or the shelters.

Ralph dropped down in the sand.

"We'll have to make a new list of who's to look after the fire."

"If you can find them."

He looked round. Then for the first time he saw how few biguns there were and understood why the work had been so hard.

"Where's Maurice?"

Piggy wiped his glass again.

"I expect . . . no, he wouldn't go into the forest by himself, would he?"

Ralph jumped up, ran swiftly round the fire and stood by Piggy, holding up his hair.

"But we've got to have a list! There's you and me and Samneric and–"

He would not look at Piggy but spoke casually.

"Where's Bill and Roger?"

Piggy leaned forward and put a fragment of wood on the fire.

"I expect they've gone. I expect they won't play either."

Ralph sat down and began to poke little holes in the sand. He was surprised to see that one had a drop of blood by it. He examined his bitten nail closely and watched the little globe of blood that gathered where the quick was gnawed away.

Piggy went on speaking.

"I seen them stealing off when we was gathering wood. They went that way. The same way as he went himself."

Ralph finished his inspection and looked up into the air. The sky, as if in sympathy with the great changes among them, was different today and so misty that in some places the hot air seemed white. The disc of the sun was dull silver as though it were nearer and not so hot, yet the air stifled.

"They always been making trouble, haven't they?"

The voice came near his shoulder and sounded anxious. "We can do without 'em. We'll be happier now, won't we?"

Ralph sat. The twins came, dragging a great log and grinning in their triumph. They dumped the log among the embers so that sparks flew.

"We can do all right on our own, can't we?"

For a long time while the log dried, caught fire and turned red hot, Ralph sat in the sand and said nothing. He did not see Piggy go to the twins and whisper to them, nor how the three boys went together into the forest.

"Here you are."

He came to himself with a jolt. Piggy and the other two were by him. They were laden with fruit.

"I thought perhaps," said Piggy, "we ought to have a feast, kind of."

The three boys sat down. They had a great mass of the fruit with them and all of it properly ripe. They grinned at Ralph as he took some and began to eat.

"Thanks," he said. Then with an accent of pleased surprise, "Thanks!"

"Do all right on our own," said Piggy, "It's them that haven't no common sense that make trouble on this island. We'll make a little hot fire–"

Ralph remembered what had been worrying him.

"Where's Simon?"

"I don't know."

"You don't think he's climbing the mountain?"

Piggy broke into noisy laughter and took more fruit. "He might be." He gulped his mouthful. "He's cracked."

Simon had passed through the area of fruit trees but today the littluns had been too busy with the fire on the beach and they had not pursued him there. He went on among the creepers until he reached the great mat that was woven by the open space and crawled inside. Beyond the screen of leaves the sunlight pelted down and the butterflies danced in the middle their unending dance. He knelt down and the arrow of the sun fell on him. That other time the air had seemed to vibrate with heat; but now it threatened. Soon the sweat was running from his long coarse hair. He shifted restlessly but there was no avoiding the sun. Presently he was thirsty, and then very thirsty. He continued to sit.

Far off along the beach, Jack was standing before a small group of boys. He was looking brilliantly happy.

"Hunting," he said. He sized them up. Each of them wore the remains of a black cap and ages ago they had stood in two demure rows and their voices had been the song of angels.

"We'll hunt. I'm going to be chief."

They nodded, and the crisis passed easily.

"And then–about the beast."

They moved, looked at the forest.

"I say this. We aren't going to bother about the beast."

He nodded at them.

"We're going to forget the beast."

"That's right!"

"Yes!"

"Forget the beast!"

If Jack was astonished by their fervor he did not show it.

"And another thing. We shan't dream so much down here. This is near the end of the island."

They agreed passionately out of the depths of their tormented private lives.

"Now listen. We might go later to the castle rock. But now I'm going to get more of the biguns away from the conch and all that. We'll kill a pig and give a feast." He paused and went on more slowly. "And about the beast. When we kill we'll leave some of the kill for it. Then it won't bother us, maybe."

He stood up abruptly.

"We'll go into the forest now and hunt."

He turned and trotted away and after a moment they followed him obediently.

They spread out, nervously, in the forest. Almost at once Jack found the dung and scattered roots that told of pig and soon the track was fresh. Jack signalled the

The pigs lay, bloated bags of fat, sensuously enjoying the shadows under the trees.

rest of the hunt to be quiet and went forward by himself. He was happy and wore the damp darkness of the forest like his old clothes. He crept down a slope to rocks and scattered trees by the sea.

The pigs lay, bloated bags of fat, sensuously enjoying the shadows under the trees. There was no wind and they were unsuspicious; and practice had made Jack silent as the shadows. He stole away again and instructed his hidden hunters. Presently they all began to inch forward sweating in the silence and heat. Under the trees an ear flapped idly. A little apart from the rest, sunk in deep maternal bliss, lay the largest sow of the lot. She was black and pink; and the great bladder of her belly was fringed with a row of piglets that slept or burrowed and squeaked.

Fifteen yards from the drove Jack stopped, and his arm, straightening, pointed at the sow. He looked round in inquiry to make sure that everyone understood and the other boys nodded at him. The row of right arms slid back.

"Now!"

The drove of pigs started up; and at a range of only ten yards the wooden spears with fire-hardened points flew toward the chosen pig. One piglet, with a demented shriek, rushed into the sea trailing Roger's spear behind it. The sow gave a gasping squeal and staggered up, with two spears sticking in her fat flank. The boys shouted and rushed forward, the piglets scattered and the sow burst the advancing line and went crashing away through the forest.

"After her!"

They raced along the pig-track, but the forest was too dark and tangled so that Jack, cursing, stopped them and cast among the trees. Then he said nothing for a time but breathed fiercely so that they were awed by him and looked at each other in uneasy admiration. Presently he stabbed down at the ground with his finger.

"There–"

Before the others could examine the drop of blood, Jack had swerved off, judging a trace, touching a bough that gave. So he followed, mysteriously right and assured, and the hunters trod behind him.

He stopped before a covert.

"In there."

They surrounded the covert but the sow got away with the sting of another spear in her flank. The trailing butts hindered her and the sharp, cross-cut points were a torment. She blundered into a tree, forcing a spear still deeper; and after that any of the hunters could follow her easily by the drops of vivid blood. The afternoon wore on, hazy and dreadful with damp heat; the sow staggered her way ahead of them, bleeding and mad, and the hunters followed, wedded to her in lust, excited by the long chase and the dropped blood. They could see her now, nearly got up with her, but she spurted with her last strength and held ahead of them again. They were just behind her when she staggered into an open space where bright flowers grew and butterflies danced round each other and the air was hot and still.

Here, struck down by the heat, the sow fell and the hunters hurled themselves at her. This dreadful eruption from an unknown world made her frantic; she squealed and bucked and the air was full of sweat and noise and blood and terror.

Roger ran round the heap, prodding with his spear

whenever pigflesh appeared. Jack was on top of the sow, stabbing downward with his knife. Roger found a lodgment for his point and began to push till he was leaning with his whole weight. The spear moved forward inch by inch and the terrified squealing became a highpitched scream. Then Jack found the throat and the hot blood spouted over his hands. The sow collapsed under them and they were heavy and fulfilled upon her. The butterflies still danced, preoccupied in the center of the clearing.

At last the immediacy of the kill subsided. The boys drew back, and Jack stood up, holding out his hands.

"Look."

He giggled and flicked them while the boys laughed at his reeking palms. Then Jack grabbed Maurice and rubbed the stuff over his cheeks. Roger began to withdraw his spear and boys noticed it for the first time. Robert stabilized the thing in a phrase which was received uproariously.

"Right up her ass!"

"Did you hear?"

"Did you hear what he said?"

"Right up her ass!"

This time Robert and Maurice acted the two parts; and Maurice's acting of the pig's efforts to avoid the advancing spear was so funny that the boys cried with laughter.

At length even this palled. Jack began to clean his bloody hands on the rock. Then he started work on the sow and paunched her, lugging out the hot bags of colored guts, pushing them into a pile on the rock while the others watched him. He talked as he worked.

"We'll take the meat along the beach. I'll go back

to the platform and invite them to a feast. That should give us time."

Roger spoke.

"Chief–"

"Uh–?"

"How can we make a fire?"

Jack squatted back and frowned at the pig.

"We'll raid them and take fire. There must be four of you; Henry and you, Robert and Maurice. We'll put on paint and sneak up; Roger can snatch a branch while I say what I want. The rest of you can get this back to where we were. We'll build the fire there. And after that–"

He paused and stood up, looking at the shadows under the trees. His voice was lower when he spoke again.

"But we'll leave part of the kill for . . ."

He knelt down again and was busy with his knife. The boys crowded round him. He spoke over his shoulder to Roger.

"Sharpen a stick at both ends."

Presently he stood up, holding the dripping sow's head in his hands.

"Where's that stick?"

"Here."

"Ram one end in the earth. Oh–it's rock. Jam it in that crack. There."

Jack held up the head and jammed the soft throat down on the pointed end of the stick which pierced through into the mouth. He stood back and the head hung there, a little blood dribbling down the stick.

Instinctively the boys drew back too; and the forest was very still. They listened, and the loudest noise was the buzzing of flies over the spilled guts.

Jack spoke in a whisper.

"Pick up the pig."

Maurice and Robert skewered the carcass, lifted the dead weight, and stood ready. In the silence, and standing over the dry blood, they looked suddenly furtive.

Jack spoke loudly.

"This head is for the beast. It's a gift."

The silence accepted the gift and awed them. The head remained there, dim-eyed, grinning faintly, blood blackening between the teeth. All at once they were running away, as fast as they could, through the forest toward the open beach.

Simon stayed where he was, a small brown image, concealed by the leaves. Even if he shut his eyes the sow's head still remained like an after-image. The half-shut eyes were dim with the infinite cynicism of adult life. They assured Simon that everything was a bad business.

"I know that."

Simon discovered that he had spoken aloud. He opened his eyes quickly and there was the head grinning amusedly in the strange daylight, ignoring the flies, the spilled guts, even ignoring the indignity of being spiked on a stick.

He looked away, licking his dry lips.

A gift for the beast. Might not the beast come for it? The head, he thought, appeared to agree with him. Run away, said the head silently, go back to the others. It was a joke really–why should you bother? You were just wrong, that's all. A little headache, something you ate, perhaps. Go back, child, said the head silently.

Simon looked up, feeling the weight of his wet hair,

and gazed at the sky. Up there, for once, were clouds, great bulging towers that sprouted away over the island, grey and cream and copper-colored. The clouds were sitting on the land; they squeezed, produced moment by moment this close, tormenting heat. Even the butterflies deserted the open space where the obscene thing grinned and dripped. Simon lowered his head, carefully keeping his eyes shut, then sheltered them with his hand. There were no shadows under the trees but everywhere a pearly stillness, so that what was real seemed illusive and without definition. The pile of guts was a black blob of flies that buzzed like a saw. After a while these flies found Simon. Gorged, they alighted by his runnels of sweat and drank. They tickled under his nostrils and played leapfrog on his thighs. They were black and iridescent green and without number; and in front of Simon, the Lord of the Flies hung on his stick and grinned. At last Simon gave up and looked back; saw the white teeth and dim eyes, the blood–and his gaze was held by that ancient, inescapable recognition. In Simon's right temple, a pulse began to beat on the brain.

Ralph and Piggy lay in the sand, gazing at the fire and idly flicking pebbles into its smokeless heart.

"That branch is gone."

"Where's Samneric?"

"We ought to get some more wood. We're out of green branches."

Ralph sighed and stood up. There were no shadows under the palms on the platform; only this strange light that seemed to come from everywhere at once. High up among the bulging clouds thunder went off like a gun.

"We're going to get the buckets of rain."

"What about the fire?"

Ralph trotted into the forest and returned with a wide spray of green which he dumped on the fire. The branch crackled, the leaves curled and the yellow smoke expanded.

Piggy made an aimless little pattern in the sand with his fingers.

"Trouble is, we haven't got enough people for a fire. You got to treat Samnenc as one turn. They do everything together."

"Of course."

"Well, that isn't fair. Don't you see? They ought to do two turns."

Ralph considered this and understood. He was vexed to find how little he thought like a grownup and sighed again. The island was getting worse and worse.

Piggy looked at the fire.

"You'll want another green branch soon."

Ralph rolled over.

"Piggy. What are we going to do?"

"Just have to get on without 'em."

"But–the fire."

He frowned at the black and white mess in which lay the unburnt ends of branches. He tried to formulate.

"I'm scared."

He saw Piggy look up; and blundered on.

"Not of the beast. I mean I'm scared of that too. But nobody else understands about the fire. If someone threw you a rope when you were drowning. If a doctor said take this because if you don't take it you'll die–you would, wouldn't you? I mean?"

"'Course I would."

Piggy took off his glasses, deeply troubled.

"Can't they see? Can't they understand? Without the smoke signal we'll die here? Look at that!"

A wave of heated air trembled above the ashes but without a trace of smoke.

"We can't keep one fire going. And they don't care. And what's more?" He looked intensely into Piggy's streaming face.

"What's more? Supposing I got like the others–not caring. What would become of us?"

Piggy took off his glasses, deeply troubled.

"I dunno, Ralph. We just got to go on, that's all. That's what grownups would do."

Ralph, having begun the business of unburdening himself, continued.

"Piggy, what's wrong?"

Piggy looked at him in astonishment.

"Do you mean the–?"

"No, not it . . . I mean . . . what makes things break up like they do?"

Piggy rubbed his glasses slowly and thought. When he understood how far Ralph had gone toward accepting him he flushed pinkly with pride.

"I dunno, Ralph. I expect it's him."

"Jack?"

"Jack." A taboo was evolving round that word too.

Ralph nodded solemnly.

"Yes," he said, "I suppose it must be."

The forest near them burst into uproar. Demoniac figures with faces of white and red and green rushed out howling, so that the littluns fled screaming. Out of the corner of his eye, Ralph saw Piggy running. Two figures rushed at the fire and he prepared to defend himself but they grabbed half-burnt branches and raced away along the beach. The three others stood still, watching Ralph; and he saw that the tallest of them, stark naked save for paint and a belt, was Jack.

Ralph had his breath back and spoke.

"Well?"

Jack ignored him, lifted his spear and began to shout.

"Listen all of you. Me and my hunters, we're living along the beach by a flat rock. We hunt and feast and have fun. If you want to join my tribe come and see us. Perhaps I'll let you join. Perhaps not."

He paused and looked round. He was safe from shame or self-consciousness behind the mask of his paint and could look at each of them in turn. Ralph was kneeling by the remains of the fire like a sprinter at his mark and his face was half-hidden by hair and smut. Samneric peered together round a palm tree at the edge of the forest. A littlun howled, creased and crimson, by the bathing pool and Piggy stood on the platform, the white conch gripped in his hands.

"Tonight we're having a feast. We've killed a pig and we've got meat. You can come and eat with us if you like."

Up in the cloud canyons the thunder boomed again. Jack and the two anonymous savages with him swayed, looking up, and then recovered. The littlun went on howling. Jack was waiting for something. He whispered urgently to the others.

"Go on–now!"

The two savages murmured. Jack spoke sharply.

"Go on!"

The two savages looked at each other, raised their spears together and spoke in time.

"The Chief has spoken."

Then the three of them turned and trotted away. Presently Ralph rose to his feet, looking at the place where the savages had vanished. Samneric came, talking in an awed whisper.

"I thought it was–"

"–and I was–"

"–scared."

Piggy stood above them on the platform, still holding the conch.

"That was Jack and Maurice and Robert," said Ralph. "Aren't they having fun?"

"I thought I was going to have asthma."

"When I saw Jack I was sure he'd go for the conch. Can't think why."

The group of boys looked at the white shell with affectionate respect. Piggy placed it in Ralph's hand and the littluns, seeing the familiar symbol, started to come back.

"Not here."

He turned toward the platform, feeling the need for ritual. First went Ralph, the white conch cradled, then Piggy very grave, then the twins, then the littluns and the others.

"Sit down all of you. They raided us for fire. They're having fun. But the–"

Ralph was puzzled by the shutter that flickered in his brain. There was something he wanted to say; then the shutter had come down.

"But the–"

They were regarding him gravely, not yet troubled by any doubts about his sufficiency. Ralph pushed the idiot hair out of his eyes and looked at Piggy.

"But the . . . oh . . . the fire! Of course, the fire!"

He started to laugh, then stopped and became fluent instead.

"The fire's the most important thing. Without the fire we can't be rescued. I'd like to put on war-paint and be a savage. But we must keep the fire burning. The fire's the most important thing on the island, because, because–"

He paused again and the silence became full of doubt and wonder.

Piggy whispered urgently. "Rescue."

"Oh yes. Without the fire we can't be rescued. So we must stay by the fire and make smoke."

When he stopped no one said anything. After the many brilliant speeches that had been made on this very spot Ralph's remarks seemed lame, even to the littluns.

At last Bill held out his hands for the conch.

"Now we can't have the fire up there–because we can't have the fire up there–we need more people to keep it going. Let's go to this feast and tell them the fire's hard on the rest of us. And the hunting and all that, being savages I mean–it must be jolly good fun."

Samneric took the conch.

"That must be fun like Bill says–and as he's invited us–"

"to a feast."

"meat."

"crackling."

"I could do with some meat."

Ralph held up his hand.

"Why shouldn't we get our own meat?"

The twins looked at each other. Bill answered.

"We don't want to go in the jungle."

Ralph grimaced.

"He–you know–goes."

"He's a hunter. They're all hunters. That's different."

No one spoke for a moment, then Piggy muttered to the sand.

"Meat."

The littluns sat, solemnly thinking of meat, and dribbling. Overhead the cannon boomed again and the dry palm fronds clattered in a sudden gust of hot wind.

"You are a silly little boy," said the Lord of the Flies, "just an ignorant, silly little boy."

Simon moved his swollen tongue but said nothing.

"Don't you agree?" said the Lord of the Flies, "Aren't you just a silly little boy?"

Simon answered him in the same silent voice.

"Well then," said the Lord of the Flies, "you'd better run off and play with the others. They think you're batty. You don't want Ralph to think you're batty, do you? You like Ralph a lot, don't you? And Piggy, and Jack?"

Simon's head was tilted slightly up. His eyes could not break away and the Lord of the Flies hung in space before him.

"What are you doing out here all alone? Aren't you afraid of me?"

Simon shook.

"There isn't anyone to help you. Only me. And I'm the Beast."

Simon's mouth labored, brought forth audible words.

"Pig's head on a stick."

"Fancy thinking the Beast was something you could hunt and kill!" said the head. For a moment or two the forest and all the other dimly appreciated places echoed with the parody of laughter. "You knew, didn't you? I'm part of you? Close, close, close! I'm the reason why it's no go? Why things are what they are?"

The laughter shivered again.

"Come now," said the Lord of the Flies. "Get back to the others and we'll forget the whole thing."

Simon's head wobbled. His eyes were half closed as though he were imitating the obscene thing on the stick. He knew that one of his times was coming on. The Lord of the Flies was expanding like a balloon.

"This is ridiculous. You know perfectly well you'll only meet me down there–so don't try to escape!"

Simon's body was arched and stiff. The Lord of the Flies spoke in the voice of a schoolmaster.

"This has gone quite far enough. My poor, misguided child, do you think you know better than I do?"

There was a pause.

"I'm warning you. I'm going to get angry. Do you see? You're not wanted. Understand? We are going to have fun on this island. Understand? We are going to have fun on this island! So don't try it on, my poor misguided boy, or else–"

Simon found he was looking into a vast mouth. There was blackness within, a blackness that spread.

"Or else," said the Lord of the Flies, "we shall do you? See? Jack and Roger and Maurice and Robert and Bill and Piggy and Ralph. Do you see?"

Simon was inside the mouth. He fell down and lost consciousness.

❒

Chapter

6

In the Land of Flies

Over the island the build-up of clouds continued. A steady current of heated air rose all day from the mountain and was thrust to ten thousand feet; revolving masses of gas piled up the static until the air was ready to explode. By early evening the sun had gone and a brassy glare had taken the place of clear daylight. Even the air that pushed in from the sea was hot and held no refreshment.

Colours drained from water and trees and pink surfaces of rock, and the white and brown clouds brooded. Nothing prospered but the flies who blackened their lord and made the spilt guts look like a heap of glistening coal. Even when the vessel broke in Simon's nose and the blood gushed out they left him alone, preferring the pig's high flavor.

With the running of the blood Simon's fit passed into the weariness of sleep. He lay in the mat of creepers while the evening advanced and the cannon continued to play. At last he woke and saw dimly the dark earth close by his cheek. Still he did not move but lay there, his face sideways on the earth, his eyes looking dully before him.

Then he turned over, drew his feet under him and laid hold of the creepers to pull himself up. When the creepers shook the flies exploded from the guts with a vicious note and clamped back on again. Simon got to his feet. The light was unearthly. The Lord of the Flies hung on his stick like a black ball.

Simon spoke aloud to the clearing.

"What else is there to do?"

Nothing replied. Simon turned away from the open space and crawled through the creepers till he was in the dusk of the forest. He walked drearily between the trunks, his face empty of expression, and the blood was dry round his mouth and chin. Only sometimes as he lifted the ropes of creeper aside and chose his direction from the trend of the land, he mouthed words that did not reach the air.

Presently the creepers festooned the trees less frequently and there was a scatter of pearly light from the sky down through the trees. This was the backbone of the island, the slightly higher land that lay beneath the mountain where the forest was no longer deep jungle. Here and there, were wide spaces interspersed with thickets and huge trees and the trend of the ground led him up as the forest opened. He pushed on, staggering sometimes with his weariness but never stopping. The usual brightness was gone from his eyes and he walked with a sort of glum determination like an old man.

A buffet of wind made him stagger and he saw that he was out in the open, on rock, under a brassy sky. He found his legs were weak and his tongue gave him pain all the time.

When the wind reached the mountain-top he could see something happen, a flicker of blue stuff against brown clouds. He pushed himself forward and the wind came again, stronger now, cuffing the forest heads till they ducked and roared. Simon saw a humped thing suddenly sit up on the top and look down at him. He hid his face, and toiled on.

The flies had found the figure too. The life-like movement would scare them off for a moment so that they made a dark cloud round the head. Then as the blue material of the parachute collapsed the corpulent figure would bow forward, sighing, and the flies settle once more.

Simon felt his knees smack the rock. He crawled forward and soon he understood. The tangle of lines showed him the mechanics of this parody; he examined the white nasal bones, the teeth, the colors of corruption. He saw how pitilessly the layers of rubber and canvas held together the poor body that should be rotting away. Then the wind blew again and the figure lifted, bowed, and breathed foully at him.

Simon knelt on all fours and was sick till his stomach was empty. Then he took the lines in his hands; he freed them from the rocks and the figure from the wind's indignity.

At last he turned away and looked down at the beaches. The fire by the platform appeared to be out, or at least making no smoke. Further along the beach, beyond the little river and near a great slab of rock, a thin trickle of smoke was climbing into the sky. Simon, forgetful of the flies, shaded his eyes with both hands and peered at the smoke. Even at that distance it was possible to see that most of the boys–perhaps all of the boys–were there."

Ralph dived into the pool. A couple of littluns were playing at the edge, trying to extract comfort from a wetness warmer than blood. Piggy took off his glasses, stepped primly into the water and then put them on

Ralph came to the surface and squirted a jet of water at him.

again. Ralph came to the surface and squirted a jet of water at him.

Ralph squirted again and missed. He laughed at Piggy, expecting him to retire meekly as usual and in pained silence. Instead, Piggy beat the water with his hands.

Piggy lay back against the sloping sand side of the pool. His stomach protruded and the water dried on it. Ralph squinted up at the sky. One could guess at the movement of the sun by the progress of a light patch among the clouds. He knelt in the water and looked round.

Long before Ralph and Piggy came up with Jack's lot, they could hear the party. There was a stretch of grass in a place where the palms left a wide band of turf between the forest and the shore. Just one step down from the edge of the turf was the white, blown sand of above high water, warm, dry, trodden. Below that again was a rock that stretched away toward the lagoon. Beyond was a short stretch of sand and then the edge of the water. A fire burned on the rock and fat dripped from the roasting pigmeat into the invisible flames. All the boys of the island, except Piggy, Ralph, Simon, and the two tending the pig, were grouped on the turf. They were laughing, singing, lying, squatting, or standing on the grass, holding food in their hands.

At this moment the boys who were cooking at the fire suddenly hauled off a great chunk of meat and ran with it toward the grass. They bumped Piggy, who was burnt, and yelled and danced. Immediately, Ralph and the crowd of boys were united and relieved by a storm of laughter. Piggy once more was the center of social derision so that everyone felt cheerful and normal.

Jack stood up and waved his spear.

His tone conveyed a warning, given out of the pride of ownership, and the boys ate faster while there was still time. Seeing there was no immediate likelihood of a pause, Jack rose from the log that was his throne and sauntered to the edge of the grass. He looked down from behind his paint at Ralph and Piggy. They moved a little farther off over the sand and Ralph watched the fire as he ate. He noticed, without understanding, how the flames were visible now against the dull light. Evening was come, not with calm beauty but with the threat of violence.

Jack spoke.

"Give me a drink."

Henry brought him a shell and he drank, watching Piggy and Ralph over the jagged rim. Power lay in the brown swell of his forearms: authority sat on his shoulder and chattered in his ear like an ape.

All of a sudden, the clouds opened and let down the rain like a waterfall. The water bounded from the mountain-top, tore leaves and branches from the trees, poured like a cold shower over the struggling heap on the sand. Presently the heap broke up and figures staggered away. Only the beast lay still, a few yards from the sea. Even in the rain they could see how small a beast it was; and already its blood was staining the sand.

Now a great wind blew the rain sideways, cascading the water from the forest trees. On the mountain-top the parachute filled and moved; the figure slid, rose to its feet, spun, swayed down through a vastness of wet air and trod with ungainly feet the tops of the high trees; falling, still falling, it sank towards the beach and the boys rushed screaming into the darkness. The parachute took the figure forward, furrowing the lagoon, and bumped it over the reef and out to sea.

Towards midnight the rain ceased and the clouds drifted away, so that the sky was scattered once more with the incredible lamps of stars. Then the breeze died too and there was no noise save the drip and trickle of water that ran out of clefts and spilled down, leaf by leaf, to the brown earth of the island. The air was cool, moist, and clear; and presently even the sound of the water was still. The beast lay huddled on the pale beach and the stains spread, inch by inch.

❐

Chapter 7

On a Hunting Spree

Ralph climbed on to the platform carefully. The coarse grass was still worn away where the assembly used to sit; the fragile white conch still gleamed by the polished seat. Ralph sat down in the grass facing the chief's seat and the conch. Piggy knelt at his left, and for a long minute there was silence.

Piggy said nothing but nodded, solemnly. They continued to sit, gazing with impaired sight at the chief's seat and the glittering lagoon. The green light and the glossy patches of sunshine played over their befouled bodies.

At length Ralph got up and went to the conch. He took the shell caressingly with both hands and knelt, leaning against the trunk.

The chief was sitting there, naked to the waist, his face blocked out in white and red. The tribe lay in a semicircle before him. The newly beaten and untied Wilfred was sniffing noisily in the background. Roger squatted with the rest.

"Tomorrow," went on the chief, "we shall hunt again."

He pointed at this savage and that with his spear.

"Some of you will stay here to improve the cave and defend the gate. I shall take a few hunters with me and bring back meat. The defenders of the gate will see that the others don't sneak in."

A savage raised his hand and the chief turned a bleak, painted face toward him.

"Why should they try to sneak in, Chief?"

The chief was vague but earnest.

"They will. They'll try to spoil things we do. So the watchers at the gate must be careful. And then–"

The chief paused. They saw a triangle of startling pink dart out, pass along his lips and vanish again.

The semicircle shuddered and muttered in agreement.

The chief's blush was hidden by the white and red clay. Into his uncertain silence the tribe spilled their murmur once more. Then the chief held up his hand.

"We shall take fire from the others. Listen. Tomorrow we'll hunt and get meat. Tonight I'll go along with two hunters–who'll come?"

Maurice and Roger put up their hands.

"Maurice."

"Yes, Chief?"

"Where was their fire?"

"Back at the old place by the fire rock."

The chief nodded.

"The rest of you can go to sleep as soon as the sun sets. But us three, Maurice, Roger and me, we've got work to do. We'll leave just before sunset."

Maurice put up his hand.

"But what happens if we meet."

The chief waved his objection aside.

"We'll keep along by the sands. Then if he comes we'll do our, our dance again."

"Only the three of us?"

Again the murmur swelled and died away.

Piggy handed Ralph his glasses and waited to receive back his sight. The wood was damp; and this was the

Together they went to the fruit trees, carrying their spears.

third time they had lighted it. Ralph stood back, speaking to himself.

Together they went to the fruit trees, carrying their spears, saying little, cramming in haste. When they came out of the forest again the sun was setting and only embers glowed in the fire, and there was no smoke.

Ralph tried indignantly to remember. There was something good about a fire. Something overwhelmingly good.

"Ralph's told you often enough," said Piggy moodily. "How else are we going to be rescued?"

"Of course! If we don't make smoke–"

He squatted before them in the crowding dusk.

"Don't you understand? What's the good of wishing for radios and boats?"

He held out his hand and twisted the fingers into a fist. "There's only one thing we can do to get out of this mess. Anyone can play at hunting, anyone can get us meat."

He looked from face to face. Then, at the moment of greatest passion and conviction, that curtain flapped in his head and he forgot what he had been driving at. He knelt there, his fist clenched, gazing solemnly from one to the other. Then the curtain whisked back.

He led the way to the first shelter, which still stood, though battered. The bed leaves lay within, dry and noisy to the touch. In the next shelter a littlun was talking in his sleep. The four biguns crept into the shelter and burrowed under the leaves. The twins lay together and Ralph and Piggy at the other end. For a while there was the continual creak and rustle of leaves as they tried for comfort.

At length, save for an occasional rustle, the shelter was silent. An oblong of blackness relieved with brilliant spangles hung before them and there was the hollow sound of surf on the reef. Ralph settled himself for his nightly game of supposition.

From the darkness of the further end of the shelter came a dreadful moaning and they shattered the leaves in their fear. Sam and Eric, locked in an embrace, were fighting each other.

Ralph continued to snigger though his chest hurt. His twitchings exhausted him till he lay, breathless and woebegone, waiting for the next spasm. During one of these pauses he was ambushed by sleep.

"Be quiet–and listen."

Ralph lay down carefully, to the accompaniment of a long sigh from the leaves. Eric moaned something and then lay still. The darkness, save for the useless oblong of stars, was blanket-thick.

"I can't hear anything."

"There's something moving outside."

Ralph's head prickled. The sound of his blood drowned all else and then subsided.

"I still can't hear anything."

"Listen. Listen for a long time."

Quite clearly and emphatically, and only a yard or so away from the back of the shelter, a stick cracked. The blood roared again in Ralph's ears, confused images chased each other through his mind. A composite of these things was prowling round the shelters. He could feel Piggy's head against his shoulder and the convulsive grip of a hand.

"Ralph! Ralph!"

"Shut up and listen."

Desperately, Ralph prayed that the beast would prefer littluns. A voice whispered horribly outside.

Something brushed against the back of the shelter. Piggy kept still for a moment, then he had his asthma. He arched his back and crashed among the leaves with his legs. Ralph rolled away from him.

Then there was a vicious snarling in the mouth of the shelter and the plunge and thump of living things. Someone tripped over Ralph and Piggy's corner became a complication of snarls and crashes and flying limbs. Ralph hit out; then he and what seemed like a dozen others were rolling over and over, hitting, biting, scratching. He was torn and jolted, found fingers in his mouth and bit them. A fist withdrew and came back like a piston, so that the whole shelter exploded into light. Ralph twisted sideways on top of a writhing body and felt hot breath on his cheek. He began to pound the mouth below him, using his clenched fist as a hammer; he hit with more and more passionate hysteria as the face became slippery. A knee jerked up between his legs and he fell sideways, busying himself with his pain, and the fight rolled over him. Then the shelter collapsed with smothering finality; and the anonymous shapes fought their way out and through. Dark figures drew themselves out of the wreckage and flitted away, till the screams of the littluns and Piggy's gasps were once more audible.

Ralph trotted down the pale beach and jumped on to the platform. The conch still glimmered by the chief's seat. He gazed for a moment or two, then went back to Piggy.

"They didn't take the conch."

"I know. They didn't come for the conch. They came for something else."

❐

The Castle Rock

Ralph was sitting with his conch in one of his hands. He was looking at the conch constantly.

"Blow the conch," said Piggy. "Blow as loud as you can."

The forests re-echoed; and birds lifted, crying out of the treetops, as on that first morning ages ago. Both ways the beach was deserted. Some littluns came from the shelters. Ralph sat down on the polished trunk and the three others stood before him. He nodded, and Samneric sat down on the right. Ralph pushed the conch into Piggy's hands. He held the shining thing carefully and blinked at Ralph.

"Go on, then."

"I just take the conch to say this. I can't see no more and I got to get my glasses back. Awful things has been done on this island. I voted for you for chief. He's the only one who ever got anything done. So now you speak, Ralph, and tell us.

"You can take spears if you want but I shall not. What's the good? I'll have to be led like a dog, anyhow. Yes, laugh. Go on, laugh."

"Piggy! Stop a minute!"

"I got the conch. I'm going to that Jack Merridew and tell him, I am."

"You'll get hurt."

"What can he do more than he has? I'll tell him what's what. You let me carry the conch, Ralph. I'll show him the one thing he hasn't got."

Piggy paused for a moment and peered round at the dim figures. The shape of the old assembly, trodden in the grass, listened to him.

"I'm going to him with this conch in my hands. I'm going to hold it out. Look, I'm going to say, you're stronger than I am and you haven't got asthma. You can see, I'm going to say, and with both eyes. But I don't ask for my glasses back, not as a favor. I don't ask you to be a sport, I'll say, not because you're strong, but because what's right's right. Give me my glasses, I'm going to say–you got to!"

Piggy ended, flushed and trembling. He pushed the conch quickly into Ralph's hands as though in a hurry to be rid of it and wiped the tears from his eyes. The green light was gentle about them and the conch lay at Ralph's feet, fragile and white. A single drop of water that had escaped Piggy's fingers now flashed on the delicate curve like a star.

At last Ralph sat up straight and drew back his hair.

They made their way to the devastated fruit trees. Piggy was helped to his food and found some by touch. While they ate, Ralph thought of the afternoon.

"We'll be like we were. We'll wash."

Sam gulped down a mouthful and protested.

"But we bathe every day!"

Ralph looked at the filthy objects before him and sighed.

"We ought to comb our hair. Only it's too long."

"I've got both socks left in the shelter," said Eric, "so we could pull them over our heads like caps, sort of."

"We could find some stuff," said Piggy, "and tie your hair back."

"Like a girl!"

They set off along the beach in formation. Ralph went first, limping a little, his spear carried over one shoulder. He saw things partially, through the tremble of the heat haze over the flashing sands, and his own long hair and injuries. Behind him came the twins, worried now for a while but full of unquenchable vitality. They said little but trailed the butts of their wooden spears; for Piggy had found that, by looking down and shielding his tired sight from the sun, he could just see these moving along the sand. He walked between the trailing butts, therefore, the conch held carefully between his two hands. The boys made a compact little group that moved over the beach, four plate-like shadows dancing and mingling beneath them. There was no sign left of the storm, and the beach was swept clean like a blade that has been scoured. The sky and the mountain were at an immense distance, shimmering in the heat; and the reef was lifted by mirage, floating in a kind of silver pool halfway up the sky.

They passed the place where the tribe had danced. The charred sticks still lay on the rocks where the rain had quenched them but the sand by the water was smooth again. They passed this in silence. No one doubted that the tribe would be found at the Castle Rock and when they came in sight of it they stopped with one accord. The densest tangle on the island, a mass of twisted stems, black and green and impenetrable, lay on their left and tall grass swayed before them. Now Ralph went forward.

Here was the crushed grass where they had all lain when he had gone to prospect. There was the neck of land, the ledge skirting the rock, up there were the red pinnacles.

Sam touched his arm.

"Smoke."

There was a tiny smudge of smoke wavering into the air on the other side of the rock.

"Some fire–I don't think."

Ralph turned.

"What are we hiding for?"

He stepped through the screen of grass on to the little open space that led to the narrow neck.

"You two follow behind. I'll go first, then Piggy a pace behind me. Keep your spears ready."

Piggy peered anxiously into the luminous veil that hung between him and the world.

Ralph moved forward on to the neck. He kicked a stone and it bounded into the water. Then the sea sucked down, revealing a red, weedy square forty feet beneath Ralph's left arm.

"Am I safe?" quavered Piggy, "I feel awful."

High above them from the pinnacles came a sudden shout and then an imitation war-cry that was answered by a dozen voices from behind the rock.

"Give me the conch and stay still."

"Halt! Who goes there?"

Ralph bent back his head and glimpsed Roger's dark face at the top.

"You can see who I am!" he shouted, "Stop being silly!"

He put the conch to his lips and began to blow. Savages appeared, painted out of recognition, edging

With ludicrous care he embraced the rock.

round the ledge towards the neck. They carried spears and disposed themselves to defend the entrance. Ralph went on blowing and ignored Piggy's terrors.

Roger was shouting.

He stood halfway along the neck and gazed at the savages intently. Freed by the paint, they had tied their hair back and were more comfortable than he was. Ralph made a resolution to tie his own back afterwards. Indeed he felt like telling them to wait and doing it there and then; but that was impossible. The savages sniggered a bit and one gestured at Ralph with his spear. High above, Roger took his hands off the lever and leaned out to see what was going on. The boys on the neck stood in a pool of their own shadow, diminished to shaggy heads. Piggy crouched, his back shapeless as a sack.

Roger took up a small stone and flung it between the twins, aiming to miss. They started and Sam only just kept his footing. Some source of power began to pulse in Roger's body.

The twins made a bolt past Ralph and got between him and the entry. He turned quickly. Jack, identifiable by personality and red hair, was advancing from the forest. A hunter crouched on either side. All three were masked in black and green. Behind them on the grass the headless and paunched body of a sow lay where they had dropped it.

Piggy wailed.

"Ralph! Don't leave me!"

With ludicrous care he embraced the rock, pressing himself to it above the sucking sea. The sniggering of the savages became a loud derisive jeer.

Jack shouted above the noise.

"You go away, Ralph. You keep to your end. This is my end and my tribe. You leave me alone."

The jeering died away.

Jack made a rush and stabbed at Ralph's chest with his spear. Ralph sensed the position of the weapon from the glimpse; he caught of Jack's arm and put the thrust aside with his own butt. Then he brought the end round and caught Jack a stinger across the ear. They were chest to chest, breathing fiercely, pushing and glaring.

"Who's a thief?"

"You are!"

Jack wrenched free and swung at Ralph with his spear. By common consent they were using the spears as sabers now, no longer daring the lethal points. The blow struck Ralph's spear and slid down, to fall agonizingly on his fingers. Then they were apart once more, their positions reversed, Jack towards the Castle Rock and Ralph on the outside towards the island.

Both boys were breathing very heavily.

There was silence again. The twins lay, inexpertly tied up, and the tribe watched Ralph to see what he would do. He numbered them through his fringe, glimpsed the ineffectual smoke.

His temper broke. He screamed at Jack.

"You're a beast and a swine and a bloody, bloody thief!"

He charged.

Jack, knowing this was the crisis, charged too. They met with a jolt and bounced apart. Jack swung with his fist at Ralph and caught him on the ear. Ralph hit Jack in the stomach and made him grunt. Then they were facing each other again, panting and furious, but unnerved by each other's ferocity. They became aware of the noise that was the background to this fight, the steady shrill cheering of the tribe behind them.

Piggy's voice penetrated to Ralph.

"Let me speak."

He was standing in the dust of the fight, and as the tribe saw his intention the shrill cheer changed to a steady booing.

Piggy held up the conch and the booing sagged a little, then came up again to strength.

"I got the conch!"

He shouted.

"I tell you, I got the conch!"

Surprisingly, there was silence now; the tribe were curious to hear what amusing thing he might have to say.

Now Jack was yelling too and Ralph could no longer make himself heard. Jack had backed right against the tribe and they were a solid mass of menace that bristled with spears. The intention of a charge was forming among them; they were working up to it and the neck would be swept clear. Ralph stood facing them, a little to one side, his spear ready. By him stood Piggy still holding out the talisman, the fragile, shining beauty of the shell. The storm of sound beat at them, an incantation of hatred. High overhead, Roger, with a sense of delirious abandonment, leaned all his weight on the lever.

Ralph heard the great rock before he saw it. He was aware of a jolt in the earth that came to him through the soles of his feet, and the breaking sound of stones at the top of the cliff. Then the monstrous red thing bounded across the neck and he flung himself flat while the tribe shrieked.

The rock struck Piggy a glancing blow from chin to knee; the conch exploded into a thousand white fragments and ceased to exist. Piggy, saying nothing, with no time for even a grunt, traveled through the air sideways from the rock, turning over as he went. The rock bounded twice and was lost in the forest. Piggy fell forty feet and landed on his back across the square red rock in the sea. His head opened and stuff came out and turned red. Piggy's arms and legs twitched a bit, like a pig's after it has been killed. Then the sea breathed again in a long, slow sigh, the water boiled white and pink over the rock; and when it went, sucking back again, the body of Piggy was gone.

This time the silence was complete. Ralph's lips formed a word but no sound came.

Suddenly Jack bounded out from the tribe and began screaming wildly.

"See? See? That's what you'll get! I meant that! There isn't a tribe for you any more! The conch is gone."

He ran forward, stooping.

❒

Chapter 9

The Hunters' Cry

Ralph lay in a covert, wondering about his wounds. The bruised flesh was inches in diameter over his right ribs, with a swollen and bloody scar where the spear had hit him. His hair was full of dirt and tapped like the tendrils of a creeper. All over he was scratched and bruised from his flight through the forest. By the time his breathing was normal again, he had worked out that bathing these injuries would have to wait.

Ralph listened. He was not really far from the Castle Rock, and during the first panic he had thought he heard sounds of pursuit. But the hunters had only sneaked into the fringes of the greenery, retrieving spears perhaps, and then had rushed back to the sunny rock as if terrified of the darkness under the leaves. He had even glimpsed one of them, striped brown, black, and red, and had judged that it was Bill.

The afternoon died away; the circular spots of sunlight moved steadily over green fronds and brown fiber but no sound came from behind the rock. At last Ralph wormed out of the ferns and sneaked forward to the edge of that impenetrable thicket that fronted the neck of land. He peered with elaborate caution between branches at the edge and could see Robert sitting on guard at the top of the cliff. He held a spear in his left hand and was tossing up a pebble and catching it again with the right. Behind him a column of smoke rose thickly, so that Ralph's nostrils flared and his mouth dribbled. He wiped his nose and mouth with the back of his hand and for the first time since the morning felt hungry. The tribe must be sitting round the gutted pig, watching the fat ooze and burn among the ashes. They would be intent.

Another figure, an unrecognizable one, appeared by Robert and gave him something, then turned and went back behind the rock. Robert laid his spear on the rock beside him and began to gnaw between his raised hands. So the feast was beginning and the watchman had been given his portion.

Ralph saw that for the time being he was safe. He limped away through the fruit trees, drawn by the thought of the poor food yet bitter when he remembered the feast.

He argued unconvincingly that they would let him alone, perhaps even make an outlaw of him. But then the fatal unreasoning knowledge came to him again. The breaking of the conch and the deaths of Piggy and Simon lay over the island like a vapour. These painted savages would go further and further.

When he had eaten, he went towards the beach. The sunlight was slanting now into the palms by the wrecked shelter. There was the platform and the pool. The best thing to do was to ignore this leaden feeling about the heart and rely on their common sense, their daylight sanity. Now that the tribe had eaten, the thing to do was to try again. And anyway, he couldn't stay here all night in an empty shelter by the deserted platform. His flesh crept and he shivered in the evening sun. No fire; no smoke; no rescue. He turned and limped away through the forest towards Jack's end of the island.

The slanting sticks of sunlight were lost among the branches. At length he came to a clearing in the forest where rock prevented vegetation from growing. Now it was a pool of shadows and Ralph nearly flung himself behind a tree when he saw something standing in the center; but then he saw that the white face was bone and that the pig's skull grinned at him from the top of a stick.

He walked slowly into the middle of the clearing and looked steadily at the skull that gleamed as white as ever the conch had done and seemed to jeer at him cynically. An inquisitive ant was busy in one of the eye sockets but otherwise the thing was lifeless.

Little prickles of sensation ran up and down his back. He stood, the skull about on a level with his face, and held up his hair with two hands. The teeth grinned, the empty sockets seemed to hold his gaze masterfully and without effort.

When the green glow had gone from the horizon and night was fully accomplished, Ralph came again to the thicket in front of the Castle Rock. Peeping through, he could see that the height was still occupied, and whoever it was up there had a spear at the ready.

He knelt among the shadows and felt his isolation bitterly. They were savages it was true; but they were human, and the ambushing fears of the deep night were coming on.

He rubbed his cheek along his forearm, smelling the acrid scent of salt and sweat and the staleness of dirt. Over to the left, the waves of ocean were breathing, sucking down, then boiling back over the rock.

Ralph put his head down on his forearms.

There were sounds coming from behind the Castle Rock. Listening carefully, detaching his mind from the swing of the sea, Ralph could make out a familiar rhythm.

The tribe was dancing. Somewhere on the other side of this rocky wall there would be a dark circle, a glowing fire, and meat. They would be savoring food and the comfort of safety.

Ralph put his head down on his forearms and accepted this new fact like a wound. Samneric were part of the tribe now. They were guarding the Castle Rock against him. There was no chance of rescuing them and building up an outlaw tribe at the other end of the island. Samneric were savages like the rest; Piggy was dead, and the conch smashed to powder.

At length the guard climbed down. The two that remained seemed nothing more than a dark extension of the rock. A star appeared behind them and was momentarily eclipsed by some movement.

Ralph edged forward, feeling his way over the uneven surface as though he were blind. There were miles of vague water at his right and the restless ocean lay under his left hand, as awful as the shaft of a pit. Every minute the water breathed round the death rock and flowered into a field of whiteness. Ralph crawled until he found the ledge of the entry in his grasp. The lookouts were immediately above him and he could see the end of a spear projecting over the rock.

He heard a cry and a flurry from the rock. The twins had grabbed each other and were gibbering.

"It's me, Ralph."

Terrified that they would run and give the alarm, he hauled himself up until his head and shoulders stuck over the top. Far below his armpit he saw the luminous flowering round the rock.

Words could not express the dull pain of these things. He fell silent, while the vivid stars were spilt and danced all ways.

As he prepared to let himself down the cliff, Ralph snatched at the last possible advantage to be wrung out of this meeting.

"I'll lie up close; in that thicket down there," he whispered, "so keep them away from it. They'll never think to look so close."

The footsteps were still some distance away.

Roger sharpened a stick at both ends. Ralph tried to attach a meaning to this but could not. He used all the bad words he could think of in a fit of temper that passed into yawning. How long could you go without sleep? He yearned for a bed and sheets–but the only whiteness here was the slow spilt milk, luminous round the rock forty feet below, where Piggy had fallen. Piggy was everywhere, was on this neck, was become terrible in darkness and death. If Piggy were to come back now out of the water, with his empty head–Ralph whimpered and yawned like a littlun. The stick in his hand became a crutch on which he reeled.

Then he tensed again. There were voices raised on the top of the Castle Rock. Samneric were arguing with someone. But the ferns and the grass were near. That was the place to be in, hidden, and next to the thicket that would serve for tomorrow's hideout. Here–and his hands touched grass–was a place to be in for the night, not far from the tribe, so that if the horrors of the supernatural emerged one could at least mix with humans for the time being, even if it meant.

He squatted down in the tall grass, remembered the meat that Sam had given him, and began to tear at it ravenously. While he was eating, he heard fresh noises– cries of pain from Samneric, cries of panic, angry voices. What did it mean?

Someone besides himself was in trouble, for at least one of the twins was catching it. Then the voices passed away down the rock and he ceased to think of them. He felt with his hands and found cool, delicate fronds backed against the thicket.

He was awake before his eyes were open, listening to a noise that was near. He opened an eye, found the mold an inch or so from his face and his fingers gripped into it, light filtering between the fronds of fern. He had just time to realize that the age-long nightmares of falling and death were past and that the morning was come, when he heard the sound again. It was an ululation over by the seashore– and now the next savage answered and the next. The cry swept by him across the narrow end of the island from sea to lagoon, like the cry of a flying bird. He took no time to consider but grabbed his sharp stick and wriggled back among the ferns. Within seconds he was worming his way into the thicket; but not before he had glimpsed the legs of a savage coming towards him. The ferns were thumped and beaten and he heard legs moving in the long grass.

At last he examined the thicket itself. Certainly no one could attack him here–and moreover he had a stroke of luck. The great rock that had killed Piggy had bounded into this thicket and bounced there, right in the center, making a smashed space a few feet in extent each way. When Ralph had wriggled into this he felt secure, and clever. He sat down carefully among the smashed stems and waited for the hunt to pass.

Ralph picked up his stick and prepared for battle. But what could they do? It would take them a week to break a path through the thicket; and anyone who wormed his way in would be helpless. He felt the point of his spear with his thumb and grinned without amusement. Whoever tried that would be stuck, squealing like a pig.

Ralph put his fingers in his mouth and bit them. There was only one other rock up there that they might conceivably move; but that was half as big as a cottage, big as a car, a tank. He visualized its probable progress with agonizing clearness–that one would start slowly, drop from ledge to ledge, trundle across the neck like an outsize steamroller.

Ralph put down his spear, then picked it up again. He pushed his hair back irritably, took two hasty steps across the little space and then came back. He stood looking at the broken ends of branches.

He caught sight of the rise and fall of his diaphragm and was surprised to see how quickly he was breathing. Just left of center his heart-beats were visible. He put the spear down again.

Something boomed up on the red rock, then the earth jumped and began to shake steadily, while the noise as steadily increased. Ralph was shot into the air, thrown down, dashed against branches. At his right hand, and only a few feet away, the whole thicket bent and the roots screamed as they came out of the earth together. He saw something red that turned over slowly as a mill wheel. Then the red thing was past and the elephantine progress diminished toward the sea.

Ralph knelt on the plowed-up soil, and waited for the earth to come back. Presently the white, broken stumps, the split sticks and the tangle of the thicket refocused. There was a kind of heavy feeling in his body where he had watched his own pulse.

Ralph fastened his hands round the chewed spear and his hair fell. Someone was muttering, only a few yards away toward the Castle Rock. He heard a savage say "No!" in a shocked voice; and then there was suppressed laughter. He squatted back on his heels and showed his teeth at the wall of branches. He raise his spear, snarled a little, and waited.

Once more the invisible group sniggered. He heard a curious trickling sound and then a louder crepitation as if someone were unwrapping great sheets of cellophane. A stick snapped and he stifled a cough. Smoke was seeping through the branches in white and yellow wisps, the patch of blue sky overhead turned to the color of a storm cloud, and then the smoke billowed round him.

Someone laughed excitedly, and a voice shouted.

"Smoke!"

He wormed his way through the thicket towards the forest, keeping as far as possible beneath the smoke. Presently he saw open space, and the green leaves of the edge of the thicket. A smallish savage was standing between him and the rest of the forest, a savage striped red and white, and carrying a spear. He was coughing and smearing the paint about his eyes with the back of his hand as he tried to see through the increasing smoke. Ralph launched himself like a cat; stabbed, snarling, with the spear, and the savage doubled up. There was a shout from beyond the thicket and then

Ralph was running with the swiftness of fear through the undergrowth. He came to a pig-run, followed it for perhaps a hundred yards, and then swerved off. Behind him the ululation swept across the island once more and a single voice shouted three times. He guessed that was the signal to advance and sped away again, till his chest was like fire. Then he flung himself down under a bush and waited for a moment till his breathing steadied. He passed his tongue tentatively over his teeth and lips and heard far off the ululation of the pursuers.

There were many things he could do. He could climb a tree; but that was putting all his eggs in one basket. If he were detected, they had nothing more difficult to do than wait. A nearer cry stood him on his feet and immediately he was away again, running fast among thorns and brambles. Suddenly he blundered into the open, found himself again in that open space–and there was the fathom-wide grin of the skull, no longer ridiculing a deep blue patch of sky but jeering up into a blanket of smoke. Then Ralph was running beneath trees, with the grumble of the forest explained. They had smoked him out and set the island on fire.

The fire was a big one and the drum-roll that he had thought was left so far behind was nearer. Couldn't a fire outrun a galloping horse? He could see the sun-splashed ground over an area of perhaps fifty yards from where he lay, and as he watched, the sunlight in every patch blinked at him. This was so like the curtain that flapped in his brain that for a moment he thought the blinking was inside him. But then the patches blinked more rapidly, dulled and went out, so that he saw that a great heaviness of smoke lay between the island and the sun.

If anyone peered under the bushes and chanced to glimpse human flesh it might be Samneric who would pretend not to see and say nothing. He laid his cheek against the chocolate-coloured earth, licked his dry lips and closed his eyes.

Someone cried out. Ralph jerked his cheek off the earth and looked into the dulled light. They must be near now, he thought, and his chest began to thump. Hide, break the line, climb a tree–which was the best after all? The trouble was you only had one chance.

Now the fire was nearer; those volleying shots were great limbs, trunks even, bursting. The fools! The fools! The fire must be almost at the fruit trees–what would they eat tomorrow?

The cries, suddenly nearer, jerked him up. He could see a striped savage moving hastily out of a green tangle, and coming toward the mat where he hid, a savage who carried a spear. Ralph gripped his fingers into the earth.

Ralph fumbled to hold his spear so that it was point foremost; and now he saw that the stick was sharpened at both ends.

A herd of pigs came squealing out of the greenery behind the savage and rushed away into the forest. Birds were screaming, mice shrieking, and a little hopping thing came under the mat and cowered.

Five yards away the savage stopped, standing right by the thicket, and cried out. Ralph drew his feet up and crouched. The stake was in his hands, the stake sharpened at both ends, the stake that vibrated so wildly, that grew long, short, light, heavy, light again.

The savage peered into the obscurity beneath the thicket. You could tell that he saw light on this side and on that, but not in the middle–there. In the middle was

A naval officer stood on the sand, looking down at Ralph in wary astonishment.

a blob of dark and the savage wrinkled up his face, trying to decipher the darkness.

Ralph screamed, a scream of fright and anger and desperation. His legs straightened, the screams became continuous and foaming. He shot forward, burst the thicket, was in the open, screaming, snarling, bloody. He swung the stake and the savage tumbled over; but there were others coming towards him, crying out. He stumbled over a root and the cry that pursued him rose even higher. He saw a shelter burst into flames and the fire flapped at his right shoulder and there was the glitter of water. Then he was down, rolling over and over in the warm sand, crouching with arm to ward off, trying to cry for mercy.

He staggered to his feet, tensed for more terrors, and looked up at a huge peaked cap. It was a white-topped cap, and above the green shade of the peak was a crown, an anchor, gold foliage. He saw white drill, epaulettes, a revolver, a row of gilt buttons down the front of a uniform. A naval officer stood on the sand, looking down at Ralph in wary astonishment. On the beach behind him was a cutter, her bows hauled up and held by two ratings. In the stern-sheets another rating held a sub-machine gun.

The officer looked at Ralph doubtfully for a moment, then took his hand away from the butt of the revolver.

"Hullo."

Squirming a little, conscious of his filthy appearance, Ralph answered shyly.

"Hullo."

The officer nodded, as if a question had been answered.

"Are there any adults–any grown-ups with you?"

Dumbly, Ralph shook his head. He turned a halfpace on the sand. A semicircle of little boys, their bodies streaked with coloured clay, sharp sticks in their hands, were standing on the beach making no noise at all.

"Fun and games," said the officer.

The fire reached the coconut palms by the beach and swallowed them noisily. A flame, seemingly detached, swung like an acrobat and licked up the palm heads on the platform. The sky was black.

The officer grinned cheerfully at Ralph.

"We saw your smoke. What have you been doing? Having a war or something?"

Ralph nodded.

The officer inspected the little scarecrow in front of him. The kid needed a bath, a haircut, a nose-wipe and a good deal of ointment.

Ralph looked at the officer dumbly. For a moment he had a fleeting picture of the strange glamour that had once invested the beaches. But the island was scorched up like dead wood. Simon was dead. The tears began to flow and sobs shook him. He gave himself up to them now for the first time on the island; great, shuddering spasms of grief that seemed to wrench his whole body. His voice rose under the black smoke before the burning wreckage of the island; and infected by that emotion, the other little boys began to shake and sob too. And in the middle of them, with filthy body, matted hair, and unwiped nose, Ralph wept for the end of innocence, the darkness of man's heart, and the fall through the air of the true, wise friend called Piggy.

The officer, surrounded by these noises, was moved and a little embarrassed.

❐

Questions Based on the Story

Chapter 1

Ralph on an Uninhabited Island

Q.1 Where did Ralph find himself after the shipwreck?
Q.2 What was the nickname of the fat boy whom Ralph met on the island?

Chapter 2

A Blazing Fire

Q.1 What did the boys make out of the heap of dead wood?
Q.2 What happened when the fire turned into a blaze?

Chapter 3

Beasts from Water and Air

Q.1 Who was made chief on the deserted island?
Q.2 Which beasts from water and air threatened the party of friends?

Chapter 4

Coming across Strange Creatures

Q.1 How was the view on the other side of the island?
Q.2 What did Ralph dream?

Chapter 5

Darkness All Around

Q.1 Why was Piggy indignant?

Q.2 When Ralph looked up into the air, what changes did he notice in the sky?

Chapter 6

In the Land of Flies

Q.1 What did the party of friends experience in the land of flies?

Q.2 Where was the beast lying?

Chapter 7

On a Hunting Spree

Q.1 Whom did the party of friends hunt?

Q.2 What were dark figures on the island?

Chapter 8

The Castle Rock

Q.1 Where was the Castle Rock situated?

Q.2 Who stabbed at Ralph's chest with his spear ?

Chapter 9

The Hunters' Cry

Q.1 What sounds of pursuit had Ralph heard?

Q.2 Whom did Ralph meet and what did he say to him?

❑❑❑

www.ingramcontent.com/pod-product-compliance
Lightning Source LLC
LaVergne TN
LVHW010115170826
845678LV00012B/2425

* 9 7 8 8 1 3 1 0 1 7 2 9 6 *